The cattle drive

Little by little the sun came up.
Some of the cattle began to stamp and
   snort.
One of the men got up and put his
   sleeping bag in his saddle pack.
Then he lit a fire and put the kettle on.

1

'Time to get on. Wake up!' called the man.
He got out some tin mugs with a rattle and
made some strong, black coffee.
In the middle of the sleeping men was a
boy. 'Wake up, Carl!' said the man.

This was the first time Carl had been on
a cattle drive.
It had been hard with such a big herd.
'Do you want some coffee?' the man asked.
'Yes please, Dad,' said Carl.

Carl got up, and went to his horse.
Carl's horse was called Raffles.
He put a saddle on Raffles and then put
   a strap round the saddle pack.
He stroked Raffles on her muzzle.

It was time to go.
'Go, go, go,' called the men.
The herd of cattle began to run.
'Hold them! Stop them!' yelled Carl's dad.
'Don't let them run!'

It was hot in the saddle.
Carl felt the sun scorch his back.
The heat gave him a thirst so he took a
   drink from his water bottle.
'Don't drink it all,' said his dad.

In the middle of the morning, they came to
   a wide creek.
It took time to drive the cattle across.
Carl was glad. It gave him time to
   paddle in the cool water.

Then a steer ran off from the herd.
'Catch it,' called Carl's dad. 'Don't let
   it run too far.'
Carl dug his spurs into Raffles.
'Come on, girl,' he said. 'Let's get it.'

The steer had big wide horns.
Carl got his rope round the horns and
   the steer went down.
The men gave three cheers. 'You did that
   like a real cowboy,' they said.

At last the cattle were safe at
   the Big 'R' Ranch.
'It was a hard drive,' said Carl's dad.
'Do you want to come next time?'

Carl could not forget the dust and the dirt.
He could not forget the heat and his thirst,
  nor the smell of the cattle.
'Do I want to come again?' he said.
'Yes please!'

Stardust

Tara sat on the rail of the horse pen.
Tara's dad had a horse on the end of
  a long cord.
The horse trotted round and round.

At last the horse stopped and Dad gave
   it a pat.
'Come on Tara,' he called. 'Bring that
   saddle over and put it on the horse.'

The horse was quite still so Tara put
    the saddle on.
But as soon as Dad let go, it gave a
    snort and kicked out its legs.
Then it ran round and round.

In the end it stopped running and
    Dad took hold of its bridle.
'It's time to get in the saddle,' Dad said.
'It won't like you on its back at first.'

As soon as Tara got on the horse, it
kicked and bucked.
Carl ran up to the rail to see.
'Hold on, Tara,' he called. 'You can do it!'

The horse crashed into the side of the pen.
Tara hit her leg and cracked her
  arm against the rails.
It hurt a lot, but Tara held on.
At last the horse stood still.

Everyone gave Tara a cheer.
The horse tossed its head, but it
   didn't buck or kick.
'She is my horse now,' said Tara.
'I think I will call her Stardust.'

Dust storm

Dad looked at the sun.
It had turned dark red.
'Look at that sun,' he said.
'It means that there is a dust storm
   on the way.'

Carl and Tara looked across the plain.
Far off they could see the dust storm.
Dad opened the big doors of the barn.
'Get all the horses in,' he said.
'Then get inside the house.'

It was not long before the dust storm
   hit the Big 'R' Ranch.
The wind shook the house and slapped
   against the barn.
The dust got in everywhere.

At last the dust storm was over.
'Now it's time to clean up,' said Dad.
He gave Carl a dustpan and brush and
he gave Tara a broom and duster.
'Get dusting,' he said.

There was dust everywhere.
Carl and Tara went outside to see.
There was dust all over the ground.
There was dust in piles in every corner.

Then it began to rain.
'Oh good,' said Tara, 'This rain will
    wash all the dust away.'
'But not inside the house,' said Dad,
    'so keep dusting'.

Printed in Hong Kong